12/12 10x

4/12

# JACK and the GIANT Barbecue

BY **ERIC A. KIMMEL**

ILLUSTRATED BY **JOHN MANDERS**

MARSHALL CAVENDISH CHILDREN

# ONCE UPON A TIME
there was a boy named Jack who loved barbecue. He would ride his pony across the mountains of West Texas for a taste of really fine ribs or sausage.

One day Jack asked his mother, "Ma, how come all we ever have for dinner are beans and tamales? How come you never cook barbecue?"

"I can't," Jack's mother told him. "Whenever I smell barbecue, I think of your daddy. Then I start crying. I can't eat barbecue with my whole plate full of tears."

"What happened to Daddy? You never told me," Jack said.

"I guess you're old enough to hear the story," Jack's mother said, dabbing at her eyes. "Your daddy made the finest barbecue in West Texas. He won every barbecue contest there was.

Then one day a giant came along. He ate up all our barbecue and stole Daddy's barbecue book, the one with all his secret recipes. It broke Daddy's heart to lose that book. He just keeled over and died. From then on I couldn't stand to taste barbecue again."

Jack made a vow right on the spot. "I'll find that giant—wherever he is—and take back my daddy's recipe book. If I don't do it, may I never taste a bit of barbecue again!"

Jack set out the next day.

All the storybooks said that giants live way above the clouds. The only way Jack knew to get that high was to climb Mount Pecos, the tallest mountain in West Texas. Jack rode his pony to the foot of the mountain.

Then he began climbing.

Jack climbed until he reached the mountaintop. He stepped onto the clouds and started walking. Soon he began smelling something smoky and sweet, with just the right hint of vinegar and spices. Barbecue! Jack followed the barbecue smell as it grew stronger and stronger.

It led to a beat-up old shack as big as a football field and as tall as a ten-story building. The sign on the front should have read GIANT'S BARBECUE, but the *G* and the *cue* had dropped off long ago. Now all it said was . . . IANT'S BARBE. . . .

The rest of the place didn't look much better. Shingles were falling off the roof. The windows were broken. The door drooped on its hinges. The patio and parking lot were a sea of trash.

"A tornado hitting this dump would be an improvement!" Jack exclaimed.

He pushed open the door and walked inside.

The inside looked even worse. Grease dripped down the walls. Rib bones carpeting the floor crunched under Jack's boots as he stepped up to the counter.

"Hello? Anybody home?" Jack called out.

"Only me, lonesome and blue. Unless you're looking for the giant. But I don't think you want to be here when he shows up."

The voice came from the jukebox in the corner.

"That giant stole my daddy's recipe book,"
Jack told the jukebox. "I aim to get it back. Will you
help me?"

"Count on me to stand by my man . . . or boy," the
jukebox said. "I hate that giant. He promised me a mansion
on the hill. Said I'd be the happiest girl in the whole USA.
Instead, I ended up somewhere over the rainbow. He won't even
listen to my music anymore." The jukebox shed a tear. "You bet I
know where your book is. It's tucked between my 45s in slot D-9.
Right between 'Your Cheatin' Heart' and 'Pancho and Lefty.'"

Jack climbed inside the jukebox. He reached inside slot D-9.
But before he could get his fingers on the recipe book, he heard a
pickup pull into the parking lot. A mighty big pickup!

"It's the giant. You've got a tiger by the tail, boy!" the jukebox told Jack.

Jack hid behind the records. The shack's walls shook as the giant came stomping in. He sniffed the air.

*Fee-fi-fo-fum!*

*A Texas boy this way has come.*

*I'll dip him in salsa and pico de gallo,*

*And swallow him down for Cinco de Mayo.*

"You're crazy!" said the jukebox. "Crazy for thinkin' anybody'd come in here. What you smell is trash! Why don't you clean it up? It's givin' me the honky-tonk blues."

"Aw, shut your tater trap!" roared the giant. "I'll tell you what. I'm hungry! What's for supper?" He opened the smoker and took out two sides of beef, ten racks of ribs, and fifty feet of sausage! He washed everything down with two dozen pitchers of sweet tea.

The giant tossed his trash on the floor. Then he leaned back in his chair and closed his eyes. Soon he was snoring like a summer thunderstorm.

"Did you get the book?" the jukebox asked Jack.

"I see it, but I can't reach it," Jack said. "I'll need more time."

"Funny how time slips away. You better not be here when the giant wakes up," the jukebox said. "Get me out of here, and you can look for it later."

"How can I do that?" Jack asked.

"These giant rib bones are the size of skis. The floor is slick with grease.
Put me on a couple of ribs, slide me out the door, and give me a push. It'll
be like skiing down Mount Pecos," the jukebox said.

Jack did just that. He hopped on, and off they went.

"The race is on," sang the jukebox.

About then the giant woke up with a hankering for barbecue. "Where's my recipe book?" he growled. That's when he noticed the jukebox was gone. He saw the rib bone tracks across the greasy floor leading to the cloud outside. It didn't take him long to figure out what had happened.

When he did, he turned hotter than a pepper sprout. He jumped in his pickup and went tearing across the clouds after Jack.

But Jack and the jukebox were flying. They zoomed right through the hole in the cloud and slid down the side of Mount Pecos, all the way to the ground.

The giant saw the hole, too. But he was going too fast to brake. That giant pickup roared through the clouds and smashed all the mountains in West Texas flat. Since then West Texas has been flat as a skillet all the way to New Mexico.

As for Jack, he opened his own barbecue shack. He serves the best barbecue in West Texas. The giant works for him. It was the only way he could get decent barbecue. Ma waits tables. The jukebox plays Hank, Patsy, Willie, and all the greatest country hits.

If you're ever in West Texas, drop by. It's not hard to find. Turn left when you see the sign. You can't miss it. Just look for . . .

To Vicki Krebsbach, Sue Kuentz, and all my friends in Texas  —E.A.K.

For Lisa and Don—and their award-winning, authentic,
no-beans cowboy chili!  —J.M.

## A NOTE FROM THE AUTHOR

Barbecue is meat—slow cooked over charcoal and seasoned with endless varieties of sauces, rubs, and marinades. My favorite barbecue is Texas barbecue, especially when you get it at a beat-up shack out in the country with sawdust on the floor, a jukebox playing Willie Nelson, and pickups lined end to end in the parking lot. *Jack and the Giant Barbecue* is my own original version loosely based on the traditional English tale "Jack and the Beanstalk." —E.A.K.

Text copyright © 2012 by Eric A. Kimmel
Illustrations copyright © 2012 by John Manders

Marshall Cavendish Corporation
99 White Plains Road
Tarrytown, NY 10591
www.marshallcavendish.us/kids

Library of Congress Cataloging-in-Publication Data

Kimmel, Eric A.
Jack and the giant barbecue / by Eric A. Kimmel ; illustrated by John
Manders. — 1st ed.
p. cm.
Summary: When Jack's mother tells him how his father died when a giant
stole his barbecue recipes, Jack vows to find the giant and retrieve the
book. Includes an author's note about Texas barbecue.
ISBN 978-0-7614-6128-9 (hardcover) — ISBN 978-0-7614-6129-6 (ebook)
[1. Barbecuing—Fiction. 2. Giants—Fiction. 3. Texas—Fiction.] I.
Manders, John, ill. II. Title.

PZ7.K5648Jac 2012
[E]—dc23
2011016402

The illustrations are rendered in Winsor & Newton Designers' gouache
with some colored pencil accents and highlights.

Book design by Anahid Hamparian
Editor: Margery Cuyler

Printed in Malaysia (T)
First edition
10 9 8 7 6 5 4 3 2 1

Marshall Cavendish
Children